Footprints in the Snow

by

Maggie Holman

Run Jump Jive

First published as 'A Cat for Christmas' 2012
This edition 2015

A catalogue record for this book is available from the
British Library
ISBN 978-90-820089-1-3

Cover design by Nik @ Book Beaver
Printed and bound by Drukkerij Zaansprint
Zaanweg 21, 1521 DK Wormerveer, Netherlands

For Roxy, John &
Jordan, the shining
stars in my sky

Chapter 1

It was almost Christmas and school had broken up for the holidays. This year the family was leaving London behind to stay with Jamie's grandfather – his Grancher Pete – in the Forest of Dean. First of all, Jamie was going to stay with his grandfather by himself, while his Mum went to Paris with her boyfriend Paul, and then they would get back on Christmas Eve. Jamie had never stayed with Grancher Pete without his Mum, and now he'd got it into his head that he would also end up spending Christmas on his own there – that Paul and his Mum wouldn't be back in time. He wasn't happy.

"I don't know why I can't come with you to Paris," he moaned. "Why do I have to go to Grancher's? I've never stayed there on my own before."

His Mum, Lyn, was busy pushing and shoving the last of Jamie's clothes into a small suitcase. She forced the lid shut and tried to click the fasteners, but then gave up. She stood up, hands on hips, and looked over to where Jamie was sitting on the wide bedroom window sill. She smiled patiently.

"Look, Jamie. We've been through this a hundred times, haven't we? You won't *be* on your own for Christmas! Paul and I will be back on Christmas Eve, as I keep telling you, and then we'll all be staying with Grancher Pete together. Paul just thought it would be nice to take me off on my own for a few days. Is there anything wrong with that? You're ten years old now. Have we ever been away on our own like this before?"

Jamie shook his head 'no' and stared down at the bedroom carpet. While he wasn't watching, Lyn sneaked quietly round the bed, grabbed him tightly and started to tickle him.

"I suppose you think I should slave over a hot stove all the time, is that it?" she laughed. "All work and no play? Well, when I get back I will be, or are *you* cooking Christmas dinner this year?"

Jamie laughed. He did love his Mum, and of course he wanted her to have a lovely time in Paris, but what he didn't want to tell her was that he was nervous about staying without her in the same cottage that his Dad had lived in when he was a child.

"Here," said his Mum, interrupting his thoughts. "Help me get this suitcase closed, and then we're done. Have you packed everything you want to take? Oh, and no Playstation, OK? You can live without it for a few days."

Lyn winked teasingly at Jamie and he stuck his tongue out at her, then he jumped down off the window sill, threw his rucksack over his shoulder and helped his Mum to fasten his suitcase. They pulled the suitcase along the landing and down the stairs, and then they left it in the hallway, beside Lyn's larger one. Next to the suitcases - and of much more interest to Jamie – was a carrier bag full of Christmas presents. In the kitchen, they collected the drinks and sandwiches that Lyn had put together for the journey, and Jamie helped to put everything into a carrier bag. Just then they heard the sound of a car pulling up outside, followed by a loud, excited honking on the car's horn.

"There's Paul now. Come on, then. We've got to make sure we drop you off in time to check in at the airport by five. Let's hope the traffic's not too bad on the motorway!"

Lyn opened the front door and they both

watched Paul as he jumped out of his huge 4x4 and bounced up the path. While Jamie looked on, Paul grabbed Lyn romantically round the waist and shouted, in a silly French accent "'Ere I am, ma cherie, ready to wheesk you away to ze sights an sounds of gay Paree!" When Lyn laughed and pushed him away, he turned to Jamie and shouted in the same silly accent "Hey, Jaymee, ow'z eet going?" He play punched Jamie's arm hard and Jamie, well used to this behaviour, lunged at him so that they fell in a heap together and started to wrestle on the carpet. Lyn watched them, arms folded, waiting.

"Come on, you two. Stop messing around. We haven't got time for this, have we? We have to go!"

Paul stood up first and started to pull Jamie to his feet, then he suddenly picked Jamie up round his waist and turned him upside down.

"Shout 'give in'!" Paul cried out, as Lyn groaned at more silly behaviour.

"No!" Jamie giggled.

"Yes! Come on – Give in. Give in! Now," Paul laughed, "before you faint!"

"OK! I give in!" Jamie replied, and Paul turned him over again and stood him on his feet.

Jamie liked Paul a lot. He always made sure he play punched and wrestled with Jamie like this when he first arrived at the house. It was Paul who'd turned Jamie into an outdoor boy and helped him to be confident. He was always thinking of things for them to do, like camping, fishing and sailing. He helped Jamie with his homework, took him swimming every Wednesday and came to watch him play football on Sundays. Jamie knew it wasn't the same as having his Dad around, but for the last two years he'd got used to Paul being there instead and he liked the idea that he was part of their family.

Outside, Jamie helped Paul to pack the suitcases and the carrier bag of presents into the boot of the 4x4. He climbed up into the back seat. He was looking forward to sitting up high and having a good view of everything as they travelled along. Paul was in the driving seat now, the engine running and raring to go, while Lyn stood at the front door with her hand on the latch.

"Right – last chance, Jamie," she called. "Are you quite sure you've got everything?"

Jamie was about to shout "Yes" when he stopped suddenly and called "No. Wait!" He jumped out of the car, ran past his Mum, through the door and up the stairs. Once in his bedroom, he pulled a shoe box out from under his bed. This was Jamie's 'secrets' box, where he kept his most important things. Amongst his collection of photos, marbles, shells and football medals, he found what he was looking for – a small black velvet bag, fastened firmly with a tasselled drawstring. He quickly returned to the car, climbed back in and put the bag inside his rucksack. Paul turned to Jamie and smiled.

"Everything OK, mate?"

Jamie nodded, as his Mum locked their front door, climbed up into the front passenger seat next to Paul, fastened her seat belt and they were off.

At first the journey out of London was boring. For the first forty minutes or so they crawled through the familiar traffic of south east London, stopping and starting continuously at traffic lights and swerving now and then to avoid other impatient drivers. Once out of London they joined the busy M25.

"It's motorway all the way now, Jamie," Paul called out over his shoulder. "The M25 first and then the M4. Boring, eh? Nothing to see but miles and miles of traffic."

They stopped only once, at the half-way point of their journey, and ate their packed lunches in the motorway services car park. As they set off again, Jamie settled down with his comics and his bag of sweets. Paul was right. There was nothing even vaguely interesting to look at out of the car window. As Jamie read quietly to himself, he was aware of the quiet buzz of voices, of Paul and his Mum chatting in the background as he read.

"Jamie. Ja…mie."

Jamie was woken gently by his Mum's singsong voice calling his name. He sat up suddenly, confused, and heard her laugh.

"You've dozed all the way!" she commented. "Look. We're in the Forest."

When Jamie looked out of the window he saw that they were no longer on the motorway, that they were now driving along a smaller, quieter road which was winding along through a pretty countryside view. Occasionally they drove past houses and cottages covered in ivy, painted in bright colours, which stood by themselves on the side of the road, but it was the famous forest which dominated the view on both sides. Wherever Jamie looked, all he could see were trees, stretching away in all directions. The boring flat motorway had been replaced by a road which twisted and turned, rising steeply uphill and then falling downhill again as they travelled further and further into the forest. Eventually they came to a stretch of straighter road.

"Just here," said Lyn.

Paul slowed down, indicated right and pulled over to the central line. He waited for a break in the oncoming traffic, then he turned off the main road and up a single dirt track.

"This is more like it! Just the job for my 4x4," he laughed, as they jostled and wobbled their way along the bumpy, untreated track. Jamie knew from his previous visits that his grandfather's stone cottage stood by itself at the end of this track, deep in the trees and hidden from the main road. He looked ahead with a mixture of excitement and trepidation. They drove until they were completely surrounded by trees, and when Paul turned a final bend, the familiar dry-stone wall appeared before them, marking the boundary of Grancher Pete's garden.

"There!" Jamie called out before he could stop himself. He quickly took in the view of the garden. His rope swing, which he'd tied up there last summer, was still hanging in the huge apple tree, but the wide lawn was bare and muddy. The dark dead winter shrubs had lost their leaves, leaving only brittle sticks. The row of wooden sheds still sat in the far corner. Paul swung in through the gate and they parked on the drive.

"Yes, we're here," said Lyn, "and look."

She pointed to an old man who stood on the doorstep of the cottage, waving at them.

"There's your Grancher, waiting for us at the door."

Chapter 2

"Hello! Hello!" Grancher Pete's voice boomed across the garden as they climbed out of the 4x4. "Come on in. I've already got the kettle on. Heard you coming."

Jamie followed his Mum through the front door and into the hallway while Paul followed behind, carrying Jamie's suitcase and the bag of presents. Jamie started to feel a little nervous again. It was eighteen months since he and his Mum had last stayed, during the summer of the previous year, and everything seemed strange, both familiar and unfamiliar at the same time.

"Come into the kitchen! Don't just stand about like you're just visiting! You know where everything is!"

Lyn looked down at Jamie and smiled, pushing him gently.

"Go on in and say hello," she said

quietly.

Jamie went on ahead, crossed the entrance hall and turned left. Once inside the kitchen, with its roaring open fire, he felt better. He looked across at Grancher Pete, who was busy pulling mugs out of one of the kitchen cupboards.

"Hello Jamie. How are you, lad? Come over here and let me see how much you've grown."

Jamie looked at his grandfather's familiar rosy round face and silvery hair. He walked towards him and was instantly wrapped up in a tight bear hug.

"Yes, you're definitely taller," said his grandfather, as he held Jamie at arm's length to get a better look at him.

"And Pete - this is Paul," said Lyn.

This was the first time Paul had come out to the cottage, and he was standing quietly in the background of the family scene.

"Hello, Paul. Jamie's told me a lot about you."

"Nice to meet you," said Paul, as he walked over to shake Pete's hand. "I've heard a lot about you too."

Grancher Pete ruffled Jamie's hair and was quiet for a moment.

"Well, I hope Jamie likes to come and stay. It's always lovely to see him."

Jamie felt nervous again, sensing a tension he couldn't understand. He was confused. One minute happy, the next afraid. Why did he feel like this?

"Right then, drinks," continued Grancher Pete. "What would you all like?"

"Coffee for me," said Lyn.

"And me," said Paul. "Coffee's great."

"Can I go to the bathroom?" Jamie asked suddenly.

"Of course. Carry on. You know where

15

it is."

Going to the bathroom was just an excuse. Jamie really wanted to look around the cottage while his Mum was still there. He headed up the stairs. At the top of the creaky wooden staircase, a narrow passage ran the length of the cottage. On the right, three wide windows looked out across the trees. On the left were the doors leading first to the bathroom, and then, further on, to a row of three bedrooms. Jamie always slept in the end room, with a view over the garden. He peeped around the door of his room and was pleased to find it looked exactly the same as it had last year. The same single bed, chest-of-drawers and wicker chair looked friendly and comforting. The cream flowered curtains were closed and the winter sun, low in the sky, shone through them, bathing the room in an inviting glow.

On the way back down the passage Jamie stopped at his grandfather's room. The door was slightly ajar. He paused for a moment and then pushed it open. He walked quietly inside and looked around. Just like his own room, his grandfather's room was full of old furniture. In one corner was a sturdy double bed. Next to it was a bedside table with a lamp. The shade was frilled and faded, and looked like it belonged to another era. Two wardrobes, kept apart by a chest-of-drawers, stood up against another wall. Jamie noticed three framed photographs sitting on the mantelpiece. As he walked over to have a closer look, he realised that he'd seen them before. They were the photographs that usually sat downstairs on the window sill in the sitting room, and Jamie wondered why they'd been moved up here.

One photograph was of Grancher Pete

with his wife, Granny Mary, on their wedding day. Jamie had never met Granny Mary because she'd died before he was born. He stared at the ancient black and white photograph, an image from another time, and he could see they both looked very happy. The next photograph was of a young Granny Mary in the garden, with a smiling fat baby on her knee. Jamie already knew that this was his Dad, Jim. He was their only child. In the third photograph his Dad was grown up, looking just the way Jamie remembered him. He was sitting beside Grancher Pete on some rocks, with a river in the background. Next to them lay their fishing rods and his Dad was holding up a large fish. His Grancher and Dad both grinned at the camera, pleased with themselves. Jamie stared at all three photographs over and over again. He had seen them lots and lots of times before, but this time he felt different about them, without being able to explain why.

"So, this is where you are! I thought you were quiet!"

Jamie jumped when Lyn's voice broke the stillness of the room. He'd been so deep I thought that he hadn't heard her come in. She walked across and stood behind him.

"Mum?"

"Hmmm?"

"Do I look like Dad?"

Lyn put her arms around her son's shoulders and pulled him close. She gazed at the photographs.

"Oh, very much. Just as handsome. Just as wonderful."

"I miss him," Jamie said quietly.

"So do I, all the time," said Lyn, "but I have you to remind me of him."

She swung her son around and kept her hands firmly on his shoulders as she looked at him.

"You do know your Dad is with us all the time, watching over us."

Jamie looked at the photographs again.

"You really think so?"

"I know so."

Jamie paused before he spoke again.

"You have to go now, don't you?"

Lyn nodded.

"We'll be back in four days' time on Christmas Eve. We'll call you every day from Paris and we'll bring you back a surprise. I promise, Jamie, so you don't need to fret. You enjoy a nice few days on your own with your Grancher."

Lyn hugged Jamie close to her and they went back down to the kitchen, where Paul was sitting with Grancher Pete. They were chatting quietly together. Paul took Jamie's suitcase up to his room, and then everyone hugged each other goodbye. Jamie stood with his grandfather at the front door, watching Paul and his Mum climb back into the 4x4. His Mum wound down the window and called out "Enjoy yourselves in the forest!" and "We'll call you when we get there!" Grancher Pete squeezed Jamie's shoulder reassuringly as they waved the couple off on their exciting French trip and the 4x4 sped off down the lane. Once they disappeared round the corner, Grancher Pete laughed out loud.

"Right then, lad," he chuckled. "To work. I've got something I need a hand with before it gets dark."

"What?" said Jamie forlornly. He didn't want to do any *work* while he was here!

"Why, the Christmas decorations, of course!"

It was only now, when his grandfather mentioned it, that Jamie realised there weren't any decorations around the cottage.

He hadn't noticed their absence when he first arrived.

"I thought you might like to help, so I waited for you before I did anything. OK with you?"

"OK," Jamie replied eagerly, relieved that his grandfather didn't actually mean *real* work!

"Right. First things first. Follow me, out to the garage."

Puzzled, Jamie followed Grancher Pete outside, then watched as he pulled open the garage doors.

"I got the tree delivered yesterday. I asked for an extra-large one this year because I have guests, and I want to show off!"

He winked at Jamie mischievously.

"Woah!" Jamie gasped when he saw the tree stretched out on the garage floor. It was easily two meters high, with a healthy spread of branches. It was much bigger and broader than the artificial tree they always put up at home in London, and much more exciting.

'Big, isn't it?" beamed Pete.

"Huge! Where are we going to put it?"

"In the corner of the sitting room, at the bottom of the stairs. Come on, then. Grab an end."

Together the two of them lifted and pulled, then lifted and pulled some more. The tree was awkward to carry and they had to stop every few feet for a rest. Jamie thought they'd never manage to get the tree inside the cottage, but eventually they were through the front door. Jamie bent the smaller top branches back so they could force the tree round the corner and then they were through into the sitting room. Grancher Pete had already prepared a large bucket in the corner, full of wet soil. They pushed and pulled hard until the tree stood straight up and they were able to ease it into its new home. Jamie watched as his grandfather tied some rope around the middle of its trunk, wrapped the rope around the banister four times to keep the tree upright and then secured it with a large knot. This held the tree firmly in place and the two of them stepped back to survey their work.

"What do you think, lad?"

"It looks even bigger now it's in here!"

"Yes, and bare, poor thing."

Grancher Pete disappeared upstairs and came back down carrying a large cardboard box. Jamie went over to help and they put the box down on the carpet. Jamie opened it and looked at the collection of Christmas decorations. As he began to explore the contents of the box, his grandfather walked over and sat down in the armchair next to the fire which roared in the sitting room hearth. He warmed his hands up close to the flames.

"Go on, lad. You can decorate the tree. I'll just sit back and watch."

Jamie found this more enjoyable than he first expected. Carefully he took out the different decorations one at a time and sorted them into piles. He found gold and silver angels with delicate wings, bells hanging from bright red ribbons, jolly Santa faces, glittering snowflakes and real pine cones sprayed with gold and silver paint. At the bottom of the box he discovered strings of red, gold and silver beads and shining baubles which spun around, reflecting the firelight as they turned. After Jamie decided where to put the decorations on the lower branches, Grancher Pete produced a small step ladder and then held onto Jamie while he reached up to decorate the higher branches he couldn't reach by himself. Finally, they placed a huge gold star on the top and hung tinsel and streamers across the ceiling. Their job was complete.

Next Grancher Pete made an evening meal of fish and chips. They sat together in the front of the television, plates balanced on their knees. Grancher Pete looked across at Jamie.

"So, do you think you'll enjoy yourself here?" he asked quietly.

"Yes, thank you," Jamie replied.

"I've been thinking of things we can do. I'm not going to make you work all the time!"

He winked at Jamie.

"I've got a few things lined up, and…" he paused mid-sentence for effect and then spoke grandly, "I have a secret that I thought I'd share with you tomorrow."

That got Jamie interested.

"What sort of secret?"

"Well, if I told you, it wouldn't be a secret any more, would it? It's something I've been spending quite a bit of time on recently. You know I'm always looking for new hobbies to fill my days. It's a bit dark to show you now, because we have to go out to the garden sheds, but I'll show you first thing in the morning."

Jamie was intrigued.

"You up for it?"

Jamie nodded and his grandfather smiled.

"Good. I was hoping you'd be interested."

They spent the rest of the evening watching television. Later, after his Mum phoned to say they'd arrived safely in Paris, Jamie said goodnight to his grandfather and went up to his room. He took the drawstring bag out of his rucksack and placed it carefully under his pillow, then he pulled the wicker chair over to the window and opened the curtains. He turned off the light and curled up in the chair, looking out across the darkness of the garden and the forest beyond. All around, the world was still, while the stars twinkled above the trees. Jamie sat there quietly, trying to imagine what the secret might be that was waiting for him in the morning.

Chapter 3

Jamie slept soundly, tired after the long journey from London and from the mixed emotions of his first evening at the cottage. When he woke up next morning it was still dark. He lay quietly in bed, watching the pink morning sun as it began to light up the room. He heard Grancher Pete get up and go downstairs, then heard him filling the kettle in the kitchen. Jamie wasn't sure what he was supposed to do, without Lyn there to tell him. Eventually he decided to get up. When he climbed out from under his quilt he discovered just how cold it was. He dressed quickly and went downstairs. In the kitchen, Grancher Pete was raking the ash from the previous night's fire out of the fireplace. He turned when he heard the kitchen door open.

"Hey, lad. Good morning! Sleep

alright?"

Jamie nodded yes and walked sheepishly into the room.

"You can give me a hand if you like. We'll get the fire going and warm ourselves up, then we'll have breakfast."

Jamie took the scuttle out to the coal shed, filled it and hauled it back inside. Grancher Pete had already filled the empty grate with fresh newspapers, firelighters and sticks. Now he lit the firelighters and Jamie watched the flames take hold. Soon the fire was blazing away and the room instantly felt warmer. Grancher Pete straightened up and rubbed his back.

"We won't put coal on it yet. Let it get going first, let it breathe. Right then, breakfast. I always have bacon and porridge when it's cold like this. Sound alright?"

Jamie wasn't sure.

"I don't think I've ever had porridge," he

admitted.

"Well, there's a first time for everything, and I haven't got any of those fancy chocolate cereals."

Pete winked again.

"Alright," Jamie said after a quick consideration. "I'll give it a try."

Grancher Pete clapped Jamie good-humouredly on his back.

"Come on then."

After they'd both eaten giant helpings of porridge, along with bacon, beans and fried bread, Jamie helped his grandfather to wash up, watching him all the time out of the corner of his eye.

"Right. You still want me to show you my secret?"

Jamie nodded excitedly.

"This way, then. Follow me!"

Jamie followed his grandfather along the stone path which cut across the lawn to the

cluster of wooden sheds which stood in the
corner of the garden. They stopped at the
first shed, which stood out from the others.
It was newer, smarter and tidier, unlike the
others which were old and worn, eaten away
by years of bad weather and woodworm.
Jamie watched his grandfather as he
unlocked a heavy padlock on the shed door
and then stepped back.

"After you!"

Jamie walked into the shed. It was quite
small, with a single window next to the
door, the sort of shed people used for
storing bikes or garden tools. The first thing
he noticed was an old wooden desk placed
under the window, with a plastic garden
chair tucked in underneath. The desk was
covered in a disorganized pile of books,
newspapers and magazines. An assortment
of pens, pencils, scissors, glue and drawing
pins lay strewn across the work surface, and

the waste paper bin was full of screwed-up pieces of paper and sweet wrappers.

Jamie surveyed all the different things on the desk and decided they weren't particularly interesting. What really caught his attention was the display which covered the shed walls. Jamie gazed at the random collection of photographs, newspaper cuttings, magazine articles, pencil sketches, lists and scribbled post-it notes, which all seemed to be about one thing – a panther. Headlines such as 'Visitors Frightened by Sighting of Black Cat', 'Forest of Dean Panther Seen Again' or 'Delivery Boy Terrified on Evening Paper Round' jumped out at Jamie from all directions. He examined the various photographs; some were pictures of the big cat, usually showing the animal as a blur in the distance, walking across a field or lying in the sun. Others showed groups of people pointing at footprints and smiling at the camera. One, horribly, was of a sheep which looked like it had been attacked and eaten. Jamie turned to his grandfather.

"Is there a panther here? In the forest? A real panther?"

His grandfather laughed.

"Well, some people say there is, and some people say there isn't, and some people just don't like to say, but there's plenty of stories about people who say they've seen something."

"Cool!" said Jamie as he gazed around the shed walls.

"Well, anyway," his grandfather continued, "this is a new hobby of mine, see? I collect things I read or hear people say about the panther and keep it all in here, and every day I go out in the woods to walk about and explore, hoping to find something to prove it's real."

"But what if you really saw it? Would you run away?"

"Oh, no. You mustn't run away from any big cat. That'd be a sure way for you to get chased. You run off making a lot of fuss, shouting and waving your arms about, and the panther will think you're its next dinner."

Jamie looked at his grandfather for a moment and then realized he was being teased again. They both burst out laughing.

"Seriously, though. If you ever see the panther, you should stand your ground and show it you're not scared, even if you're terrified. If you stay calm, it'll get bored and go away."

"How do you know that?"

Grancher Pete winked.

"Read it in a book."

As Jamie completed a full circle of the shed, his eyes fell on a large map of the

Forest of Dean taped to the back of the door. The map was covered in a selection of coloured drawing pins.

"What's all this about?" he asked as he studied the map.

"That's all the places where the panther's supposed to have been seen," Grancher Pete replied, and he walked over to join Jamie. He pointed to a specific area, coloured dark green to show that it was woodland.

"You can work out the different places by using the key. These smaller lines are the rambling paths. These wider lines are the cycling tracks. They're specially built for all the tourists who like to come here for the mountain biking, but lots of people use them for walking through the forest as well. See here? This is where I live, and..."

"Oh, yes!" Jamie interrupted, excited. "Look at all the pins! That means there's been a lot of sightings just near here!"

Grancher Pete smiled at Jamie's enthusiasm.

"That's right. Lots."

Jamie turned and looked at his grandfather.

"Have you seen the panther?"

"Me? No. Not yet, anyway, but that's why I go out every day to have a look. An old man like me needs something to keep him busy, Jamie, and this is my latest hobby."

Jamie looked at the map again.

"Are you going today? Can I come?"

"Of course. Come on. I'll lock up the shed and we'll get off into the woods while it's still dry. It's supposed to rain this afternoon."

Grancher Pete locked the padlock again and they set off across the garden. When they reached the back door, Jamie stopped.

"Do you show everybody your panther stuff?"

Just for a moment, Jamie thought his grandfather looked sad.

"No. I don't usually share my panther stuff with other people, so I suppose," he stopped for a second and the old twinkle was back in his eye, "I suppose that makes you important, like royalty."

He ruffled Jamie's hair affectionately and then they went inside the cottage.

Ten minutes later they were walking up the cycle track at the back of the cottage. When they came to a crossroads they turned onto one of the rambler's paths, which was more overgrown and uneven than the well-maintained cycling route, and soon they were deep in the trees. The path became narrower and they had to walk in single file. As Jamie walked at the back he found the going harder than it had been on the cycle track and he slipped about in the mud. The thick twisted roots of the ancient trees burst through the ground as if they were deliberately waiting to trip him up. Now and then his wellington boots sank unexpectedly into the mud, so that he had to pull hard to get them out and keep up with his grandfather.

"Why didn't we just stay on the cycle track?" he moaned after a while, when he slipped yet again. "It was much easier!"

Up ahead, Grancher Pete turned and waited for him to catch up.

"Because we won't find anything out on the cycle track," he replied. "The panther will more likely travel through this kind of undergrowth, where it can hide and wait to attack its prey."

"Well, what about all those sightings you cut out of the newspapers? The panther wasn't seen in the trees then. Sometimes it was out on the main road or near people's houses."

"True enough," Grancher Pete agreed, "but we're still more likely to find paw prints or other evidence deep in the trees, where it's always muddy. Like here. Look!"

Suddenly Grancher Pete stopped in his tracks and this made Jamie jump in fright.

"What is it?" he whispered.

"Come and see – there."

Jamie walked over to where his grandfather was pointing at the ground.

"A print," Pete indicated.

"It doesn't look like a panther point," replied Jamie, unimpressed.

"I never said it was. No, this is a deer print – see the two halves of the hoof shape – but at least it shows you how clearly you can see things in the mud."

Jamie sighed, trying not to look bored.

"Had enough, eh?" laughed his

grandfather.

"I thought we'd find something straight away," Jamie shrugged.

"Well, why don't we head back for some lunch? We're going out later anyway."

"Are we?" Jamie almost shouted. "Where are we going? Another surprise?"

"Every Wednesday I go over to play chess with my mate Chris. I have tea with him and his missus and the kids. Thought you might like to join us while you're here."

"Oh, yes! Where do they live?"

"In the forest."

Jamie thought for a moment.

"What – you mean really in the forest?"

"Well, sort of in the forest. You'll see what I mean when we get there. We'll set off about three-thirty, before it gets properly dark, or the panther might get us!"

They both laughed and then they retraced their steps along the path, one behind the other again, back towards the cycle track.

"So, how many children are there?" Jamie asked, eager to know more about the possibility of new playmates to spend time with during his stay.

"Now, let's see," Pete began. "Caro's the eldest. She's a bit older than you. She's fourteen, then there are two little ones, Finn and Molly. Molly is the youngest."

"Oh," said Jamie, disappointed to hear that there was no-one his own age.

"They're nice kids," Pete continued. "I'm sure you'll all get along fine."

They reached the cycle track and strolled quietly back to the cottage. For a while, neither of them spoke, and Jamie listened to all the sounds of the forest around him. Now and then a branch cracked and fell to the ground. He saw several squirrels running up the trees, and the different cries of the birds broke the silence. Gradually, Jamie became aware of a different sound, away in the distance. The sound got closer and he realized it was the sound of voices, shouting and laughing. As they got even closer he could make out what they were saying. Someone was calling "Pete! Hey, Pete! Wait for us! Peeeeeeete!"

Jamie and his grandfather both turned round, and Jamie saw the strangest sight. Three children were heading towards them, each of them on a different-sized bike. Out in front, an older girl led the way on her mountain bike. Behind her, two much smaller children pedalled along, one on a smaller mountain bike and the other on an old-fashioned tricycle. What amazed Jamie about the trio was their appearance. They looked like rainbow children. None of their clothes matched; the pinks, blues, greens and oranges of their trousers, coats, hats and scarves – even their boots – all exploded in a mish-mash of clashing patterns and stripes. Jamie had never seen people dressed in this way, and to top it all, the older girl's hair was dyed a bright red. Against all the regular dull browns and greens which surrounded them, they looked completely out of place.

"Well, well," laughed Grancher Pete as the children caught up to them. "That's the magic of the forest for you, lad. You mention someone, and suddenly they appear!"

Jamie had already guessed that these were probably the three children they'd just been talking about, and he watched as they slowed up and came to a halt beside him. He suddenly felt very shy now that they were here.

"Hi, Pete," said the older girl, out of breath.

"Hello there, Caro," he replied. "This is my grandson, Jamie."

"Hi," Caro said, smiling at Jamie. "This is Finn and Molly."

Finn grinned broadly in Jamie's direction, while Molly hid behind her big sister and peeped cautiously at everyone.

"We were just on our way over to call at the cottage and we saw you from the top of the hill," Caro continued. "Mum says she hopes you're still coming over tonight, while you've got Jamie staying, because she wants you to bring Jamie to meet us all."

"Of course we're coming. I can't miss my weekly chance to beat your Dad at chess, and I think Jamie's ready for some other company."

Jamie blushed, and then he felt angry with himself for blushing. He was also embarrassed that his grandfather had guessed he might be getting bored. He looked away into the trees.

"OK, then. We'll get back and tell Mum. See you later," Caro called cheerfully, as she started to turn her bike around. "Come on, you two."

She set off back up the track, looking back to check on her brother and sister.

"Bye," said Finn, and he waved and set off after Caro. Grancher Pete laughed as Molly started to pedal her tricycle, looking back at them now and then, wobbling along and trying to keep up with the others.

"Told you they were nice kids," said Pete, as they also continued on their way. "We'll have a nice evening, eh?"

Jamie nodded a cautious agreement. There were those feelings again; excitement and worry at the same time.

Chapter 4

After lunch, Jamie went with Grancher Pete to chop logs for Edith, one of Pete's neighbours. She seemed to be much, much older than Grancher Pete and quite frail. She took a shine to Jamie and spent all afternoon following him about. She told him all about her family history – several times – and kept explaining to him that she couldn't put the logs in the wood-burning stove unless they were small enough for her to lift. When they finished the logs and were about to leave, Edith insisted on giving Jamie a huge hug and two pound coins for his Christmas money box. Finally three-thirty arrived. Jamie and his grandfather both pulled on their wellingtons and big coats.

"If you like, we could walk through the forest instead of taking the car," Pete suggested. "I thought it would be more of an adventure, because we'll have to come back through the trees in the dark."

Pete waved his super-powerful torch reassuringly in front of him, as if to persuade Jamie, but there was no need. Jamie readily agreed. He would have agreed to anything. He wanted to see Caro, Finn and Molly again, wanted to see their home in the forest. Back in London, as far as Jamie knew, everyone lived in apartment blocks, rows of terraced houses or on huge estates. He'd never heard of anyone living in a forest before!

Just as the sky was turning an atmospheric grey, a sure sign that the winter nightfall wasn't far away, Grancher Pete locked up the cottage, led Jamie back across the garden and out onto the same track they'd used that morning. This time, however, they set off in the other direction. As they walked, the daylight gave way to a dimmer and dimmer twilight, and Grancher Pete soon decided to switch on his torch. Its powerful beam shone ahead, lighting their way.

"Have you walked this way on your own before? How far is it? How long will it take us to get there?" Jamie asked.

"Depends on how fast we walk. It's not far this way, going as the crow flies instead of around the road way. If we keep this pace up, probably take us about twenty minutes."

"Will we be in time for tea? What will we do for the rest of the evening? How many games of chess do you usually play?"

"Questions! Questions!" Grancher Pete laughed. "Let's wait and see what the evening turns up. That's the best way to look at things, I always say."

After walking uphill for about ten minutes, the track began to slope away on the other side and joined a wider road which led further into the trees. Jamie could see lights in the darkness up ahead.

"Do you come up here every week?" he asked next.

"Oh, yes," Grancher Pete laughed. "Every Wednesday without fail, I make sure I get across for a game of chess with Chris and share some of Annie's delicious cooking. It's the best in the forest, I reckon."

They walked on in silence again.

"It's really dark now," Jamie commented.

"It certainly is. We'll be alright, lad. Don't you worry."

They followed the road as it twisted and turned. Jamie glanced nervously into the trees on either side as they walked, and then he noticed that the lights he had seen up ahead were growing brighter. As they got even closer he saw that the lights were coming from a collection of windows, all different shapes and sizes, making a pattern of square and rectangular-shaped lights against the darkness. They weren't close enough to be able to see what sort of buildings the windows might belong to, and Jamie's imagination started to run wild.

"Is this it? Is this where they live?" he asked, bewildered and excited.

"Yes. This is where they live."

The way ahead was barred by a horizontal wooden pole which had been placed across the road, making a barrier for any vehicles that might want to drive on. Jamie followed his Grancher as he skirted around the end of the pole and he found himself walking through long wet grass. He was glad he was wearing his wellingtons! When Grancher Pete stooped low to get under the lower branches of the trees, Jamie followed suit. They walked out into a large clearing. The bright moonlight was no longer restricted by the thickset dense foliage, and Jamie could see that the clearing was round in shape and very wide.

A number of vehicles were parked higgledy-piggledy around the edge, leaving a space in the centre. Some of the vehicles were static, free-standing caravans, familiar to Jamie from his summer holidays by the sea, while others looked like the large delivery vans you might see out on the road, their storage containers now converted into living space. In the shadow of the moonlight, Jamie could see collections of chairs, picnic tables and storage boxes beside each van door. Many of the curtains were closed against the night. Through those that were still open, Jamie could see people watching television, or sitting eating and talking together. Grancher Pete watched Jamie as he gazed around.

"Never seen a camp like this, have you?" he laughed.

"Never. Do they live here all the time?"

"Yes, unless they go off travelling, but most people use it as their base."

"So why didn't we come and see your friends when we stayed here last summer?"

"Because last summer they went somewhere else. They can do that – please themselves."

"Cool!" Jamie replied, obviously impressed.

"Anyway, here we are. You can see what life is like for Caro, Finn and Molly. This is their caravan."

Jamie stood back, suddenly nervous again, as Grancher Pete knocked a rat-a-tat-tat on the door of the next caravan they came to. Molly pulled back the curtain of the large window at the end and let it drop again. A moment later Caro opened the door. She smiled.

"Hi, Pete. Hello again, Jamie. Come on in."

"Hello?" Grancher Pete called cheerfully as he climbed up the metai steps outside the door. "Anyone home?"

He disappeared inside and Jamie followed, lagging behind. Inside, he discovered an interior which was definitely like the caravans they'd stayed in on holiday. They came first to a small dining area, with a galley kitchen on one side, and a wooden table and benches on the other. The benches were placed around three sides, leaving the fourth side open so people could walk past. A huge giant of a man seemed to fill one bench. He was broad-shouldered and his shirt sleeves were rolled up to reveal his strong arms. His black hair was pulled back in a ponytail and his face was covered in an enormous beard. He looked like he should be outside chopping down trees, but instead he was busy unpacking a chess set from a plastic box and setting them out on a chequered board. Finn was curled up next to him, pushing comfortably into his side, and Jamie guessed this must be their father, Chris.

"Evening, Pete," Chris boomed across the table.

"How's things? D'you want a quick game before we eat?"

"Why not? And Chris – this is Jamie."

"Hello, young fella," Chris boomed at Jamie now, and he reached out to shake Jamie's hand.

"I met Jamie already, when we were out in the forest," Finn whispered.

"So I heard. You're here for Christmas, aren't you?"

"Yes, and my Mum will be back for Christmas as well," Jamie spoke firmly and reassuringly.

"She's off to Paris for a few days with her fella," Grancher Pete added. "Gives me and Jamie a chance to spend some time together."

As Jamie glanced past his grandfather, trying to peek further into the caravan, Caro appeared at his side.

"Shall I show you round?" she asked, as if she'd read his thoughts.

"Yes, please."

By now Grancher Pete had pulled off his coat and was squeezing in next to Chris, settling himself ready for their game, and Caro led Jamie away from the dining area. In just a few short steps they arrived at the end of the caravan. They walked into a sitting room. A sofa and two matching chairs were placed around a small television set. There were windows on three sides and the curtains were closed against the darkness outside. Molly was curled up in the middle of the sofa, watching a children's programme.

"We call this our cosy corner. Hey, Molly – look. Jamie's here," said Caro, prodding her sister to get her attention. "Say hello."

Molly glanced quickly at Jamie, waved once and then turned back to the television. She started to suck her thumb.

"Hi, Molly," said Jamie, still feeling shy.

"Our bedrooms are at the other end. You wanna see them?"

"OK."

They walked back past Chris and Grancher Pete, who were already engrossed in their battle, and Jamie noticed that Finn had disappeared. Down the passage, Caro opened the first door on the left.

"The bathroom," she said, matter-of-factly, and she closed the door and carried on.

"My parents' room."

Caro pointed to the next door but didn't open it.

"Molly and Finn's room."

Caro opened this door. Jamie peeped past her and saw that it was very small, with just enough room for a pair of bunk beds on the left, and a wardrobe and chest-of-drawers on the right. Bright pictures decorated the walls. Mobiles hung from the ceiling. Two boxes of toys poked out from under the bottom bunk.

"And this is the best room," Caro announced grandly, "because it's mine! Come on in."

Caro's bedroom was situated at the opposite end of the caravan to the cosy area. A single bed stood in the corner with a small bedside table next to it. Behind the door there was a built-in wardrobe, next to that a chest-of-drawers, and in another corner there was a mis-matched desk and chair. Jamie didn't know any teenagers back in London, so he didn't know if Caro's room was typical or not, but it was certainly untidy! All the floor space was covered with clothes, bags and shoes, while every available space on the bedside table, desk and chest-of-drawers was covered in piles of books, magazines, boxes, tins and storage jars. Brightly-coloured mobiles hung here and there, and a framed poster of an angel looked reflectively down from its place of honour on the wall. Just then Jamie heard a giggle. Caro put her finger to her lips, indicating him to stay quiet. She looked around.

"Is there someone in my room?" she called out, winking at Jamie. "I hope not, or there'll be trouble!"

There was a moment of silence, and then

another giggle. Jamie couldn't help himself and he started to giggle too, although he tried hard to keep it inside. Caro crept quietly across the room and suddenly lifted up the corner of the quilt, which was hanging down over the side of the bed. She reached under and playfully pulled out a squealing Finn by his ankle. He stood up, unable to stop giggling, but Jamie was surprised to see Caro looking serious.

"You know you're not supposed to come in my room when I'm not here," she said quietly. She looked disappointed.

"I know, but I wanted to join in whatever you and Jamie were doing," Finn replied through his laughter. Just then the caravan door opened and closed again.

"Mum!" Caro called over her shoulder. "Tell Finn he can't come in my room if I'm not in it first."

Jamie looked down the passage. A small,

round lady dressed in a heavy coat was ambling towards them. Her blonde hair was pulled back in a bun and her face looked flushed and red.

"Hi, there," she smiled. "You must be Jamie. I'm Annie, everybody's Mum. Welcome. Glad you could join us for supper. Hey, Finn. Come and set table, and I keep telling you, don't go in Caro's room, or I'll tell her to go and hide in yours, and then she'll jump out and give you a fright. Anyway, I'm surprised there's anywhere to hide, Caro. Your room's such a tip!"

Annie winked at Jamie. He thought she seemed flustered and out of breath, but she wasn't about to stop for a break. In an instant she turned and headed back towards the kitchen. The children followed her.

"Can I help?" Jamie offered.

"Thank you!" Annie replied. "Just make sure Finn puts the cutlery in the right place, will you? He's got to learn. Here, you two need to put your chess game somewhere else, and hurry up!"

Grancher Pete lifted the chess board carefully, leaving the game in progress, and put it up onto a shelf behind him. In no time at all there was a hustle and bustle of cutlery, plates and glasses. Grancher Pete moved along to sit in the corner and Jamie sat next to him. There was just enough room for all seven of them – Chris, Annie, Caro, Finn, Molly, Jamie and Pete – to squeeze in together around the table.

"What's for supper?" Caro asked.

"Shepherd's pie," Annie replied as she put salt and pepper shakers next to a large jug of juice in the centre of the table and passed glasses around to everyone. "We made a giant pot of mince over at Di's, so there's probably enough for the whole camp. That's why I was a bit late."

There was just enough room on the table for a ceramic dish containing Annie's cooking, and everyone watched as she served up their meal.

"So, Jamie. What do you think of our caravan home?" Chris asked, as they all tucked in eagerly.

"It's lovely," Jamie said. "Feels really friendly."

"Different, you mean," Caro interrupted. "That's what people usually say."

She stood up and looked around, inspecting the interior.

"Well, well, well," she said in a posh voice. "This is different!"

"Stop it," Annie laughed. "Sit down and eat your food."

After they finished off the shepherd's pie, they all tucked into bowls of ice cream.

"So," Annie turned to Jamie, "is your Mum going to be back from Paris in time for Christmas?"

"Yes. They'll be back on Christmas Eve, in the morning."

"And then they're all staying til the New Year," said Grancher Pete.

"Great," said Caro. "They can come over here, can't they, Dad?"

"Of course, if they want to."

"We always have a pig roast on Christmas Night with a big bonfire in the middle of the camp," Caro continued. "Last year was brilliant. Loads of music and dancing and games."

"Who's coming back on Christmas Eve?" Finn suddenly piped up.

"Jamie's Mum and her boyfriend, Paul," Grancher Pete explained. "First time I met Paul. He seems nice, eh, Jamie?"

"Why's your Mum got a boyfriend?" Finn asked.

Pete, Chris and Annie looked at each

other.

"That's enough, Finn. Don't be nosey," Chris said gently, but Finn pressed on.

"Isn't your Mum married to your Dad?"

"Well, yes, sort of, but," Jamie stumbled over the words, "but he.."

"He what?" Finn asked, curious now.

"Finn," Chris said, a little more firmly.

"He died," said Jamie quietly.

Everyone stopped talking and looked uncomfortably at each other. Only Molly carried on eating her ice cream, having fun as she stirred it around her bowl, unaware that anything was wrong. Annie stood up.

"Finn, you have to help me clear up. Caro, maybe you could take Jamie and Molly along to your room?"

Jamie followed Caro through the caravan, relieved that nothing more had to be said about his Dad in such a public way. Molly jumped up onto Caro's bed and looked at her sister.

"Can we play snakes and ladders? Please, Caro?"

Caro laughed.

"Do you mind?" she asked, turning to Jamie. "It's a bit childish, but Molly likes it."

"That's because she's a child," Jamie observed, and they both laughed.

"Exactly! Come on then, Mol. Sit here on the floor."

Finn joined them after his chores were done and they laughed as they climbed up ladders and fell down snakes again and again, until Chris came along to say it was bedtime for the two younger children. With them gone, the room seemed quiet and empty. Jamie sat on a chair, looking around. Caro stretched out on the bed.

"Don't mind Finn," she said quietly, as if she'd been waiting for the right moment to say something. "He's young. He finds out how the world works by asking questions. He didn't mean any harm earlier."

"I know," Jamie replied. "Actually, I've also got some questions."

"Yeah?"

"Like, why've you got an angel on the wall?"

"She looks after me."

"Why?"

"Why not?"

"I mean, what's she protecting you from?"

Caro shrugged her shoulders.

"From whatever comes along."

"Do you feel protected?"

"Yes. Don't you?"

Now it was Jamie's turn to shrug.

"My Mum looks after me."

"Well," Caro continued, "her angel probably helps her to do that."

They sat in silence for a moment, Caro waiting for another question.

"Where's your computer?" Jamie asked.

"Haven't got one."

"Really?"

"Really!" Caro laughed. "There's no phone line this far out from the road, so no digital stuff for us, and there's no cable anywhere in the forest."

Caro could see that Jamie was amazed by this technical gap in her life.

"So," she began to make a list, counting on her fingers, "no computer, no phone line, no mobile phone because you can't get a signal, no television."

"But," Jamie interrupted, "Molly was watching television when I got here."

"DVD," said Caro triumphantly.

"Ah!" Jamie replied.

"Yes – ah! So I bet you're wondering what we do with our time, and don't we get

68

bored?"

"Oh, no. I didn't mean that."

"I use the computers at school, I have a mobile phone I use when I can get a signal and I watch TV when I go to my friends. I don't hang around with my baby brother and sister *all* the time! Anyway, listen. I want to show you something."

Caro walked over to one of the windows and pulled back the curtains.

"Come and look."

Jamie joined Caro and together they looked out into the darkness.

"Look at the stars," she whispered. "Do you ever just sit and look at the stars back in London?"

"Sometimes," Jamie replied, but he had to admit that the stars in London didn't seem to have the same magic as the stars that were flickering above them now.

"If I lived somewhere else," Caro

continued, "the stars wouldn't look like this, because there's something special about the stars in the forest."

They said nothing more, and sat for a while looking at the night sky, when they were interrupted by a knock on Caro's door. It was Grancher Pete.

"Come on, Jamie. I was thinking we should head back."

"OK."

A few minutes later Jamie and his grandfather were wrapped up against the cold and ready to go. Annie hugged Jamie tightly.

"What a sweetie you are!" she exclaimed.

"Well, Jamie, it was great to finally meet you. I've heard so much about you," Chris spoke next, and he shook Jamie's hand in mock formality. "Come and see us over Christmas, and bring your Mum and Paul."

"Thank you," said Jamie, overwhelmed by all the attention.

"Bye, Jamie," Caro called from where she was standing behind her parents.

The caravan door closed behind them as they waved goodbye and then Grancher Pete led Jamie towards the trees. They walked out of the clearing, back along the road and onto the cycle track, following their earlier route. Grancher Pete's torch lit up the way, but outside of its powerful beam the forest looked black and threatening. Jamie found himself wanting to walk closer to his grandfather, and his grandfather noticed. He looked down, smiled and pulled Jamie close.

"I wish my Dad was here," Jamie whispered.

Grancher Pete put an arm securely around his grandson's shoulders.

"So do I, lad," he replied. "So do I."

Chapter 5

Next morning Jamie ate his breakfast by the open fire in the kitchen. It was warm and cosy and he felt comfortable. He'd only been here for just over a day, and he was thinking about how busy he and his grandfather had been. He was actually beginning to enjoy this visit and he felt less and less anxious. He caught sight of his grandfather watching him from where he was sitting at the kitchen table, reading his newspaper. Jamie smiled at him and he smiled back. When Jamie finished his breakfast he curled up in the armchair and watched the flickering flames.

Suddenly the peaceful atmosphere was interrupted by a sharp knock on the window behind him, which made him jump. By the time he turned round to look, no-one was there, of course, and instead he heard the sound of footsteps running round the corner of the cottage. The footsteps stopped and, after a pause, the silence was followed by a loud banging on the kitchen door. Jamie listened as more footsteps ran away and were joined by the sound of suppressed giggling. Jamie looked at his grandfather, who winked and got up to answer the door. When he opened it he looked from right to left and then right again.

"Why, there's no-one there. I wonder who was knocking on the door. Must be the forest fairies. They're always playing tricks!"

He made as if to close the door again. Just then there was movement outside, and Caro, Finn and Molly all jumped out from their respective hiding places. They presented themselves at the door with a loud 'Taraah!' and Grancher Pete laughed.

"Well, well. Come in, come in! Look,

Jamie. We've got visitors, and not the fairy kind at all!"

Caro marched in first, followed by her brother and sister. They flopped down together round the kitchen table.

"What brings you here so early?" asked Grancher Pete.

"It's going to be nice and sunny today," Finn piped up.

"And so we thought we'd see if Jamie wanted to come and play in the forest," said Caro.

"We want to show him all our special places," whispered Molly, her big eyes staring mysteriously.

"Oh, can I go, Grancher? Can I? Do you mind?"

Jamie was already up out of his chair and pulling on his wellingtons.

"Of course you can go. You'll have a great time. Caro will see to that."

Caro play punched Grancher Pete affectionately and then, when Jamie was ready, they were off.

"Make sure you bring Jamie back before dark," Pete called after them. "He doesn't know the forest like you do!"

A chorus of voices called "We will!" and then all four children were gone, up over the garden wall and racing into the forest.

Once they were deep in the trees, the children slowed down to a stroll and led Jamie off the cycle track. They picked their way through brambles, tree roots and mud, walking in single file with Caro at the front. The ground ahead rose up into a gradual hill. Here the trees thinned out. In between the remaining trees, huge rocks lay scattered across the hillside.

"Let's play hide and seek. Please!" called Finn.

"Do you want to, Jamie?" Caro asked, looking across at him.

"Oh, yes. This is a great place for hide and seek."

"Can I count first?" Molly asked. Caro and Finn laughed.

"You can't count past eight yet," Finn pointed out.

"I'll count first if you like," Jamie offered.

"OK," Caro called as she grabbed Molly's hand and set off. Finn was already running in the other direction.

"That big fir tree is base," Caro called over her shoulder. "Count to a hundred."

Jamie walked over and leaned up against the tree. He covered his eyes with his hands and started to count. He counted loudly so the other children wouldn't think he was cheating.

"Ninety-seven, ninety-eight, ninety-nine,

a hundred. Coming, ready or not!" he called as he dropped his hands from his face and looked around.

For a moment the glare of the morning sun blinded him, until his eyes became used to the light again. No-one in sight, as he expected. He laughed to himself. This was fun! He set off to find the others, circling the hill and peering round the large trees and behind the rocks. When there was no sign of anyone he climbed up the hill, scrabbling for a hold on the rocks or lower branches of the trees when he slipped.

He reached the top and realised he could see all around, but still there was no sign of either Caro, Finn or Molly. This puzzled him; surely he'd see them from here? They wouldn't have gone that far. He made his way back to the fir tree base, feeling a little concerned. No-one was back at base either. Had they run off and left him?

"I give up!" he shouted loudly. "I've looked everywhere. I can't find you!"

Suddenly there was a giggle which made him jump. The giggling was joined by other voices. They sounded so close, but Jamie looked all around and still he couldn't see the children.

"Look up here," said Caro's voice.

Surprised, Jamie looked straight up above him into the fir tree, and there they all were, perched up in the branches, hidden by the dense green needles.

"I guess I lost," Jamie laughed, as he watched Finn and Caro climb nimbly down and then turn to help Molly.

"Guess so," replied Caro. "Come on. I'll show you where we went to hide. We only came back here once you walked round the side of the hill."

The children led Jamie back round the hill again, through the trees and across a small stream. Jamie hadn't gone this far when he was looking for them. They must have been fast! Now they arrived at another hill. They stopped at a huge boulder, set into the hillside and higher even than Caro, and there, hidden behind it, was an opening which disappeared into the darkness.

"Cool," said Jamie.

Without waiting for his older sister, Finn walked confidently into the opening. When Jamie followed Caro and Molly into the darkness, he discovered that they were actually in a tunnel. There was a glow of daylight up ahead, and Jamie guessed that just a little further on, the tunnel would open out into a cave. The cave was much higher and wider than Jamie had expected. The light was created by a hole in the roof which allowed a shaft of sunlight to penetrate the darkness. The light revealed pale stone walls, worn and gnarled with age and covered in moss. The walls were damp and the cave had the same earthy smell as the tunnel. In the centre, at the brightest part, four small rocks were placed evenly in a circle. Caro, Finn and Molly sat down on three of them in such a familiar way that Jamie knew they came here all the time.

"That one's yours," Finn pointed. "We pulled it over this morning, before we came to get you."

Jamie joined the others and sat down on his appointed stone. He looked around.

"This is so cool," he said. "I don't think there's anywhere like this in London, or anywhere else!"

"And when we came this morning to move your rock," said Caro, "we left a packed lunch here as well."

She walked over to a darker corner of the cave and came back with a rucksack. Inside were sandwiches, drinks and fruit.

They ate the food hungrily, and afterwards Caro reached back inside the rucksack and pulled out a giant bar of chocolate. She broke it into squares and passed them around.

"We come here all the time, don't we, kids?"

Finn and Molly nodded, their mouths full of chocolate.

"No-one ever comes here," she continued, "because no-one else knows it's here."

"Is it safe here?" Jamie asked.

"Yes," Caro snorted, as if the question were unnecessary. "Why wouldn't it be?"

Jamie shrugged. He decided he wouldn't even bother trying to explain what his life was like in London, that there were no safe secret places to play in, that his Mum would never let him play outside all day like this.

"But what about the panther? My

81

Grancher says there's a panther here. If there is, aren't you worried it might get in here? You wouldn't be safe then, and nobody could save you."

The children were surprisingly serious now.

"All the forest animals have their own space. They understand each other, don't they, Caro? If you don't bother them, they won't bother you," said Finn quietly, sounding wise beyond his years.

"What – you mean there actually is a panther living here?"

Jamie was looking at Caro, who shrugged her shoulders.

"I've never seen it myself," she replied, speaking as quietly as Finn, "but that doesn't mean it isn't there."

Suddenly Jamie felt that the atmosphere in the cave had changed, and that somehow he was delving into something private, something he wasn't part of because he didn't live here; the forest wasn't part of his everyday world. Just then his daydreaming thoughts were interrupted when Molly piped up.

"Anyway, Caro can talk to animals, so if the panther came in here, she'd tell it to leave us alone and go away."

Everybody laughed and the ice was broken. The sense of fun was back.

"What d'you mean, talk to animals?" Jamie laughed. "You mean like Dr Dolittle in the film?"

"Caro learns special things from our Gran," Finn explained. "She can talk to animals, and she can use the secret signs in the forest. Gran shows you, doesn't she, Caro? And one day she's going to show me as well."

Caro was quiet. She smiled at Finn for a moment, as if she were about to say something, but instead she jumped up from her rocky seat.

"Come on. Let's play on the rope swing, see if Jamie can stay on longer than any of us."

The children had to walk further into the trees to locate the swing. Caro climbed up a tall oak tree and unfastened it from where it was looped around a branch, out of sight. The long rope was threaded through a plank of wood to make a seat and then tied underneath in a large knot.

"Dad made it. No-one knows it's here 'cept us," Molly whispered as she tugged at Jamie's sleeve. "Another secret, like our cave."

Each of the children took a turn on the swing. They climbed up and sat on the plank while everyone else pushed, or they stood up on the plank if they were feeling more daring. Jamie and Caro helped the two younger children to hold on together, sitting side by side. Jamie couldn't believe the fun he was having, and he felt a little jealous of his new forest friends and their huge playground. Back at home, his own terraced house was surrounded by rows and rows of other houses. The only places he had to play in were their small back garden and the local park.

When Finn and Molly started to look tired, Caro suggested they head back. Jamie had no idea what time it was, but the sun wasn't far off the tops of the trees and he guessed it was late afternoon. He followed Caro again, back through the maze of trees, until they climbed out onto yet another cycle track. Caro lifted Finn up to give him a piggy back. Jamie did likewise and picked Molly up. In seconds she was fast asleep, snoring into his ear.

Caro and Jamie chatted quietly as they

walked along. Caro listened while Jamie told her all about where he lived in London. He described his house, his school, the busy, built-up areas, the parks, the constant sirens, the noisy traffic and the planes passing overhead.

"I think I would hate to live somewhere like that," Caro commented. "I'm just so used to all the open space out here."

"Have you always lived out here, in your caravan in the forest?"

"No, not always, but we've always lived in the countryside. We live here most of the year and then in the summer holidays we go off to other traveller sites, or maybe to some festivals. Last year we went to Spain, high up in the mountains. It was beautiful."

Jamie was about to ask something else when Caro suddenly whispered "Ssssh." She stopped walking and looked into the trees. Jamie couldn't see anything but trees, and he thought of the panther and felt afraid, but then Caro smiled and nodded across to her right.

"Look," she whispered.

Jamie followed Caro's gaze. At first he still couldn't see anything, then suddenly a piece of the forest seemed to move and sway. A large stag, tall and majestic, wandered out of the trees and stopped in front of them on the track. At first it nosed around on the edge, unaware of the children, but then it turned and saw them in the half-light. Jamie nervously whispered "Caro?" but before he could say anything else, she raised her hand to quiet him. She put Finn carefully down on the ground and stepped slowly towards the stag. Finn also seemed nervous, and he reached up and slid his hand through the crook of Jamie's elbow.

Together they watched as Caro reached

out gently with her left hand. Jamie heard
her make soft clicking noises with her
tongue, and now and then she made a gentle
"Sssssh" sound. Jamie thought that this was
how you would approach an animal you
weren't sure of, like the big dog at the end
of his street. Caro suddenly stopped the
clicking and shushing noises and began to
speak in an almost-whisper – strange words
he'd never heard before, words that certainly
weren't English. Jamie looked down at Finn,
who was grinning at him.

"Told you," he whispered. "Watch. Caro
will send the stag away so we can get past
and go home."

When Jamie looked back at Caro, he saw
that the stag was walking slowly towards
her. She was still holding out her left hand
and the stag nuzzled gently into it, as if it
were saying hello. Caro reached up with her
other hand and stroked the stag's broad

nose, all the while speaking in her strange language. Finally the stag turned back towards the trees. It paused and then darted off into the undergrowth, where in seconds it was lost from view. Caro looked back over her shoulder and grinned.

"That was so cool!" Jamie said, quite amazed. "You really can do that stuff, just like Finn said!"

Caro looked pleased as she walked towards them and lifted Finn onto her back again. All the way home, Jamie threw questions at her - How did she remember that strange language? Where was it from? What was she saying? - but Caro simply smiled and refused to share her secrets. When they arrived back at Grancher Pete's garden, he was waiting for them by the back gate.

"Caro spoke to a stag!" Jamie said excitedly.

"Did she now?"

Grancher Pete smiled and threw Caro a knowing glance.

"Thanks for bringing Jamie back, kids. Best jump in the car, though, Caro. I'll take you round the road way. It's too dark to be walking back with two tired little'uns."

Caro climbed in the front of the car with Pete, while Jamie sat in the back with Molly on his lap and Finn curled up next to him. In minutes they were asleep, and as Jamie thought about the wonderful day he'd had, he gradually gave in to his own deep slumber, and dreamt he was swinging through the trees on the antlers of a giant stag.

Chapter 6

A pleasant surprise was waiting for Jamie when he woke next morning. He stretched and yawned, then jumped out of bed, opened the curtains and discovered a completely white world which stretched away before him. In seconds he was dressed and downstairs, unable to contain his excitement.

"Grancher Pete! Grancher Pete! It snowed in the night! Have you seen it?"

He found his grandfather frying bacon in the kitchen. He laughed when he saw Jamie's excited face.

"Don't they have snow in London, then?"

"Yes, sometimes, but not like this."

Jamie opened the back door to get a better view.

"Can I go outside?"

"Of course. You don't need to ask, silly, but have a hot breakfast first, or you'll freeze."

Jamie wolfed down a bacon sandwich and an extra-large bowl of porridge, and minutes later he was out in the back garden, wrapped up in his wellingtons, duffle coat, hat, gloves and scarf.

Outside the snow was so deep that Jamie couldn't recognize anything. The details of the garden had disappeared under the thick snowy blanket. None of this mattered, however, because he didn't need much to build a snowman. Grancher Pete watched as Jamie patted the snow together into a small round ball which he proceeded to push around the garden. In no time at all Jamie had made a giant snowball, perfect for his snowman's fat body. While Jamie pushed a second smaller snowball around to make a head, Grancher Pete called to him across the

92

garden.

"Hey, Jamie. I'm going to pop into the village to get some extra things, in case we get snowed in properly. Come on."

Out of breath, Jamie looked across at his grandfather and then back at his half-built snowman.

"Can't I stay here?"

"Well, I…"

"Please. I want to finish my snowman."

"Alright, then. I won't be long, but listen – stay in the garden, d'you hear?"

"I will. See you in a bit."

Jamie waved when Grancher Pete honked the car horn and disappeared down the icy track, then he returned to his task. In no time his snowman was finished. Now it stood guard on the snow-covered lawn, complete with a carrot nose from Grancher Pete's vegetable box and three black teeth from the coal shed. Jamie took off his own hat and scarf and put them on the snowman.

"Pleased to meet you," Jamie said in mock formality, as he bowed to his snowy friend. He wanted to show Grancher Pete his finished work, but when he checked in the yard on the side of the cottage, he saw that Pete wasn't back yet. Jamie wasn't sure what to do next. He climbed the apple tree and looked out across the forest. Everything was shining and sparkling white as far as he could see, like a magical fairy kingdom. He climbed back down, found some tins in Grancher Pete's recycling box, stood them on the wall and tried to knock them off with snowballs. This kept him busy for a little while, but he wasn't really enjoying himself, playing on his own.

Back in the cottage, he ate some oatmeal biscuits and washed them down with a glass of milk. Where was Grancher Pete, he wondered? Shouldn't he be home by now?

He went back outside and climbed onto the garden wall, at a spot where he could see down the lane. Jamie decided to sit there and wait for his grandfather. However, after sitting still for just a few minutes, he felt his feet start to go numb. What was worse, he really was getting bored. He mulled over what to do. Perhaps he could set off down the road towards the village and surprise Grancher Pete on his way back.

His thoughts turned to Caro, Finn and Molly. He'd enjoyed the whole day yesterday when they'd played in the forest. He jumped down from the wall and ran round to the back of the garden. He looked into the trees. Grancher Pete had told him to stay in the garden, but surely it wouldn't hurt to pop across and see his new friends. He could find the way on his own. It was straight down the cycle track. Easy! He imagined Caro, Finn and Molly playing together in the snow, and what fun they'd be having, and that decided it. He left a note on the kitchen table for his grandfather. Outside the garden gate was frozen shut but that didn't stop him. He climbed over the garden wall and set off into the forest.

*

The snow covered everything, so Jamie stopped for a moment to get his bearings. Although the landscape was now completely different to how it looked the day before, he worked out roughly where he thought the cycle track would be and began to pick his way towards it. This was harder than Jamie had expected. Even though the ground was hard underneath the compact snow, now and then it gave way under his feet and he slipped downwards into hidden holes. He tripped on tree roots and broken branches that lay hidden beneath the snowy carpet, waiting to catch him out.

Jamie struggled on in this way for quite some time, and gradually he realized that the view ahead of him wasn't changing. All he could see were bare trees stretching in front of him, pointing their gnarled finger branches into the cloudy grey sky. He also began to worry. He knew that he wasn't on the cycle track. Walking wouldn't be this difficult on a man-made track. He wouldn't keep slipping on hidden obstacles. His feet felt cold in his wellingtons and his fingers started to feel the same way. He stopped for a moment to get his breath and wished he'd never set off, then suddenly, up ahead, he thought he saw something familiar.

A mound of white rose up out of the ground. His heart leapt as he hoped it was the hill they'd all been playing on the day before. Excited, he became more and more certain that if he climbed it, he'd find his new friends playing in the snow. All he had to do was get to the top. Jamie's change of heart helped him to forget the cold and he quickly set off, trying to run in short slippery steps.

Climbing the hill was the most difficult thing he'd done so far. More than once he slipped on the steep ground, where the snow prevented him from getting a good foothold. He grabbed at the lower branches of the trees to stop himself falling all the way down and eventually, in this stop-and-start way, he reached the top. Imagine Jamie's disappointment when he looked across from the summit and saw an unfamiliar scene. He looked for the large fir tree that had been their hide-and-seek base. He looked for the large boulder that hid the mouth of his friends' secret cave.

Instead of these familiar objects, Jamie

saw that the slope fell down on the other side just as sharply as the side he'd just climbed, and at the foot of the slope was a large pond. The pond water was also snow white, and Jamie guessed it must be frozen. He knew now that he had no idea where he was and that he should head back, but just then something shot out from behind a tree and caught his attention. It was a rabbit. Its brown fur stood out against the snow around it. Jamie laughed out loud when the rabbit ran straight across the frozen pond and disappeared into the trees on the other side. Jamie decided to have a closer look at the pond before he set off for home.

Slowly Jamie made his way down the slippery slope. When he reached the bottom he looked around. There was no-one to be seen. He was completely alone. What's more, for the first time he noticed how absolutely silent it was. No birds singing.

No sounds of people walking by or traffic in the distance. Jamie knew he was really deep in the trees and his earlier uncomfortable feelings returned. He had been thinking of throwing some stones across the frozen water, but now he felt that he shouldn't, that he would be disturbing the scene. And, it was really cold. He felt a coldness that was nothing to do with it being winter. This new cold came from the atmosphere by the water and Jamie was afraid. He looked around for a path to walk round the edge of the hill and pick up his tracks, intending to follow them home, and that's when he saw it.

Inside the tree line on the other side of the pond, looking sleek and black against the unspoiled snow, was the biggest cat he'd ever seen. Jamie froze on the spot as it slowly picked its way through the trees. Now and then it stopped to sniff the ground or paw at something hidden in the snow.

Jamie was terrified and fascinated at the same time. He knew this was the panther his grandfather was looking for. Oh, how he wished that Grancher Pete was here with him now. He remembered his grandfather's words when they were standing in the shed. "If you ever see the panther you should stand your ground and show it you're not scared, even if you're terrified. If you stay calm it'll get bored and go away." Then Jamie also remembered Finn's solemn words. "All the forest animals stay in their own space. If you don't bother them, they won't bother you." Now Jamie knew why he felt so spooked. He had trespassed into the panther's domain. He stood perfectly still, hoping the panther would wander past without noticing him.

Jamie's hopes were soon dashed. The panther loped slowly and silently down to the edge of the pond, straight across from where Jamie was standing. It sniffed around at the water's edge and bent down to lick at the frozen surface, and then it stopped, straightened up and looked at Jamie. They made eye contact, and Jamie knew he'd been spotted. His knees turned to jelly as he tried to think of a plan. How quickly could he climb a tree? Do panthers climb trees? Will the frozen water hold if the panther rushes at him or will it have to circle the pond first? Just at that moment, as Jamie's thoughts flew in all directions, the panther lowered itself to the ground and assumed a drawn-back threatening position, just like their neighbour's cat did when it was getting ready to pounce.

Jamie prepared himself for the worst, for an attack from this vicious wild animal, wishing he'd never left the garden, aware that he was alone and defenceless. Moving slowly, the panther turned left, staying next to the pond. Its head was low, in a hunting position, and its eyes were fixed on Jamie. Unable to move, Jamie watched as the big cat began to take careful, calculated steps, placing its paws along the water's edge. Now it was only metres away. Its warm breath made misty swirls in the cold air. Jamie saw a hint of its razor-sharp teeth as it opened its jaw, and saw the claw marks it left in the snow. He closed his eyes and thought he would faint from fear.

In that same moment he felt a movement behind him. Before he had time to turn and look, Caro appeared beside him. The panther was so close. It had stopped, ready to spring, when Caro stepped forwards, barring its way. She quickly knelt down in the snow and held her arms outstretched in front of her, the palms of her hands raised towards the animal in a gesture of defiance, and then she shouted in the same strange language Jamie had heard her use the night before when she had spoken so calmly to the stag. This time the words were not gentle and coaxing. This time they were loud words, quick, urgent and strong. Jamie watched the panther turn and run, a streak of midnight black against the snow, and then his legs gave way and he collapsed into Caro's welcoming arms.

Chapter 7

Jamie stirred from his sleep. For a moment he felt confused and wondered where he was. He slowly opened his eyes and saw bright sunlight forcing its way through cream flowered curtains. He gazed around at the familiar furniture and gradually realised he was in his bedroom at Grancher Pete's cottage. As his sleepy eyes became more focused, he turned over and saw his Mum sitting on the edge of the bed.

"Mum!" he shouted, and he sat up in bed to reach out to her. "When did you get here?"

Lyn hugged her son tightly.

"This morning, about eleven. Jamie, can you remember what happened yesterday? You wandered off in the snow and Caro found you. She raised the alarm and got you home. Apparently you've been asleep for nearly twenty-four hours."

"Oh, yes. It's Christmas Eve," Jamie remembered out loud, avoiding his Mum's question. "You said you'd get here on Christmas Eve."

"And you didn't believe me, although I don't know why, and here I am."

"Is Paul with you?" Jamie asked.

"Yes."

Lyn leaned her head on one side and looked quizzically at Jamie.

"Is that alright?" she asked.

Jamie nodded.

"I'm glad you're back, and I'm hungry," Jamie announced.

His Mum laughed.

"I'll go and find you some breakfast. You stay there and keep warm."

Lyn hugged Jamie again and he watched her close the door behind her. He leaned back into the pillows.

He felt very tired and it was nice that no-one was telling him that he should be up out of bed. As he lay there quietly, enjoying the sunshine, there was a quiet knock at the door.

"Come in," he called formally and sat up.

He heard a muffled giggle coming from behind the door, then the door opened and Molly peeped at him.

"Hello. What are you doing here?" Jamie called.

Molly laughed and bounced into the room, followed immediately by Finn and then Caro. Molly and Finn both climbed up onto the bed and sat cross-legged by Jamie's feet. Caro was carrying a tray which she laid down across Jamie's knees.

"Christmas Eve breakfast just for you!" she announced.

Jamie looked at the tray. In front of him

was a mug of steaming hot chocolate, a glass of fresh orange juice, brown bread cut into soldiers and two eggs sitting in egg cups. The eggs were dressed in home-made paper hats, coloured in with felt pens. One was a Santa Claus. The other was a snowman. Jamie laughed.

"Mum helped us make them," said Molly.

"Thanks, everyone. What a nice surprise."

Just then Grancher Pete shouted up the stairs to say that Christmas biscuits were out of the oven and ready to eat. Molly and Finn immediately rushed out of the room. Caro closed the bedroom door behind them. She sat down again and watched Jamie as he tucked into his eggs and toast.

"So, how are you feeling?" she asked.

"Alright, I suppose," Jamie paused and looked at her. "A bit confused, I think."

"What about?"

"Well, about how you knew where to find me yesterday. I knew I was completely lost in the snow."

"I was on the edge of our camp," Carc began, "collecting wood with Finn for the Christmas bonfire. Suddenly I heard a man calling my name, over and over. I looked at Finn and he didn't seem to hear the voice, so I knew it was meant just for me. I saw the man, in the distance, waving at me, so I told Finn to go home. The man had started to run and I went after him. He kept looking back, like he was checking I was there. He led me up a hill but when I reached the top, he'd disappeared. I looked for him, and that's when I saw you by the pond, and the panther about to jump at you."

"What were those words you were shouting?"

"Words my Gran taught me."

"They sounded like the words you spoke to the stag."

"Yes, but I was saying something different. Urgent words. Emergency words. But hey, that panther was huge! It must be the one your Grancher's looking for."

"I know."

"Did you tell him about it?"

"No. I think I've just been asleep."

Caro laughed.

"You'll be famous now, seeing it up so close. You should tell everyone. All the papers will come and interview you. You might even be on television!"

Jamie listened to Caro, but he wasn't laughing. He wasn't sharing her excitement.

"But Caro – where did the man go?"

"I dunno."

"You know you shouldn't have followed him, Caro. You're not supposed to follow strangers. He might have been planning to hurt you."

"But I knew I was safe."

"How?"

"Like I said, Finn didn't seem to hear him calling, and then I knew."

"Knew *what*?" Jamie was getting a bit frustrated.

"That he wasn't from 'our world', as my Gran would say."

Jamie sat quietly, considering what Caro seemed to be saying.

"I want to show you something," he said quietly.

He put his breakfast tray to one side, felt around under his pillow and pulled out the velvet bag. He unfastened the drawstring, took out a small silver photo frame and handed it to Caro. She looked at the man in the photo, dressed in an army uniform, smiling at her. She looked at it for a long time, then she turned to Jamie.

"This is your Dad, right?"

"Yes. Looks smart, doesn't he? And here."

Jamie stuck his hand inside the bag again and pulled out a small flat display box with a hinged lid. He opened it and passed it to Caro.

"This is his medal. He got it for being brave when he died, in Iraq. He was trying to save someone. I was three when it happened."

"Jamie," Caro began quietly.

"Mum wanted me to have it. I promised her I would always look after it.."

"Jamie," Caro said again, more firmly this time.

"What?"

"This is the man I followed in the snow."

Jamie stared at Caro. His lip trembled and his eyes began to fill with tears.

"But how could that be?" he whispered, his voice shaking. "And where did he go? Where did his footprints go?"

Caro shook her head and her voice was quiet.

"He didn't leave any footprints," she said slowly. "That's how I knew it was safe to follow him, that something was wrong."

"I don't understand," said Jamie, and he looked away across the room.

Caro watched him, and then reached out to squeeze his hand.

"You don't have to understand. You just have to know. Your Dad saved you, Jamie. He was there when you needed him, or that panther would've killed you."

They sat in silence.

"Caro – let's keep this a secret. Let's not tell anyone about the panther – or my Dad. Not yet, anyway."

"Alright, if that's what you want."

She smiled and stood up.

"I have to get Finn and Molly back home. They still have presents to wrap. They just wanted to see you first. I hope you can get to the bonfire tomorrow. And hey – Merry Forest Christmas."

"Thanks, Caro, and Merry Christmas."

Caro closed the bedroom door behind her. Jamie looked at his Dad's photo again. Just then a loud knock made him jump. He put the photo, medal and bag under the pillow. It was his Mum at the door. When she came in and sat on the bed, Jamie saw Paul standing in the doorway.

"Hey, mate," Paul grinned. "You've had lots of visitors this morning. Have you got time for one more?"

"Of course."

Paul came in and sat next to Lyn. He leaned forward and ruffled Jamie's hair.

"Are you OK? Sounds like you had a big

adventure yesterday, getting lost in the snow like that."

"Yes," agreed Lyn. "It was lucky for you that Caro was nearby and came across you like that. Pete says those kids know the forest like the back of their hands. They're like Indian scouts."

Jamie didn't reply. He looked from his Mum to Paul.

"Did you enjoy Paris?"

"It was big," laughed Paul.

"And cold," laughed Lyn.

"But we managed to find a cosy little café which was exactly what I was after," Paul winked, and then he and Lyn both became more serious. Lyn took Jamie's hand in hers.

"Jamie, we want to tell you something," she spoke, a little warily.

"What?"

"You do know that I love and miss your

115

Dad, and he'll always have a special place in my heart and in our home."

"And you know I wouldn't expect to take his place, or expect you to forget him," Paul continued, his voice a little choked, "I just love your Mum, and you."

"You're getting married," Jamie guessed.

Lyn and Paul smiled.

"That's why I wanted to take your Mum away on her own. I wanted to propose to her in a romantic city."

"But," said Lyn, "First we want to be sure that you're happy with our plans."

"It's great," Jamie replied, "Really great. I think Dad will be watching and think so too."

"You know I'm really proud of you," said Lyn, and she reached over to hug Jamie. "You're a special little boy."

"We'll be fine, won't we?" Paul winked.

"We'll have time to do even more stuff together."

Jamie nodded.

"Anyway," Lyn stood up as she spoke, "don't you want to know what we've brought back for you? We've got lots of tourist gifts from Paris, but we've brought you an early Christmas present as well. It's too difficult to wrap up so you can have it today. It's waiting for you downstairs."

"Is it? What is it? I'll be right down!"

Jamie jumped out of bed when Paul and Lyn left. Before he did anything, he took his Dad's photo and medal back out from under the pillow. He took the medal out of its box and turned it over, read the inscription on the back, felt the weight of it. He studied his Dad's photo. His Dad couldn't save him, because he died. Jamie knew that, but somehow his Dad was able to get a message to Caro, just when it really mattered. His

Dad really was watching over them, just like his Mum said. Jamie knew Paul would look after him and his Mum, and all the fears he'd felt at the start of the trip melted away. Now he was happy and excited.

He put the medal and the photo back in the velvet bag, then he got dressed and went downstairs.

"Hey, here he is, everyone," called Paul as Jamie walked into the kitchen, "and there's your present, Jamie, over by the fire, keeping warm."

Puzzled, Jamie walked slowly round the kitchen table. He could feel everyone's eyes on him as he approached the fireplace, where he could see a cardboard box. He heard a rustling sound. He walked carefully up to the box, peeped in and saw the tiniest, tiniest kitten he'd ever seen. It was jet black, and its huge eyes stared up at him as he bent to pick it up.

"Thank you! Thank you!" Jamie cried out, as he clutched the kitten and rushed around to hug his Mum, Grancher and Paul.

"Your Mum said you really wanted a kitten," said Paul, "so now you've got one. You should give it a name that will remind you of your Christmas in the forest."

"I will. I'm going to call it Panther."

"That's nice," said Grancher Pete, nodding and smiling in agreement. "No-one in London will have a cat with a name like that. Let's hope it doesn't grow as big!"

Everyone laughed again, and Lyn decided it was time to make them all a cup of tea.

Special thanks go to the following people for supporting me with this book:

The Saturday Morning Writing Group & Liesl Olivier at the English Bookshop, Lauriergracht, Amsterdam;

Lyndsay Gregory, Nynke Hondius, Julie Mair & Beth Young; Group 5A of 2011/12 at the Amsterdam International Community School;

Janneke Pepers, Ann Ingleby-Lewis & David Collier;

Lieke J Kessels, Roxy Holman & David Holman

And finally………
If you enjoyed this story, please leave me a review at Amazon or Goodreads, or at my website:
www.maggieholman.com

Thank you,
Maggie